Rocket

WHEEL

moon distance X rocket speed =

weight = ?

Gears
- Spoons
- forks

* and biscuits :)

Down the dark, dark stairs he tip-tip toed.

High on the top, top shelf he reeeeaaaached... nearly there...

Oliver was a good boy.
Oliver was a kind boy.
Oliver shouldn't have been
skulking, sneaking, creeping...
But he was hungry.

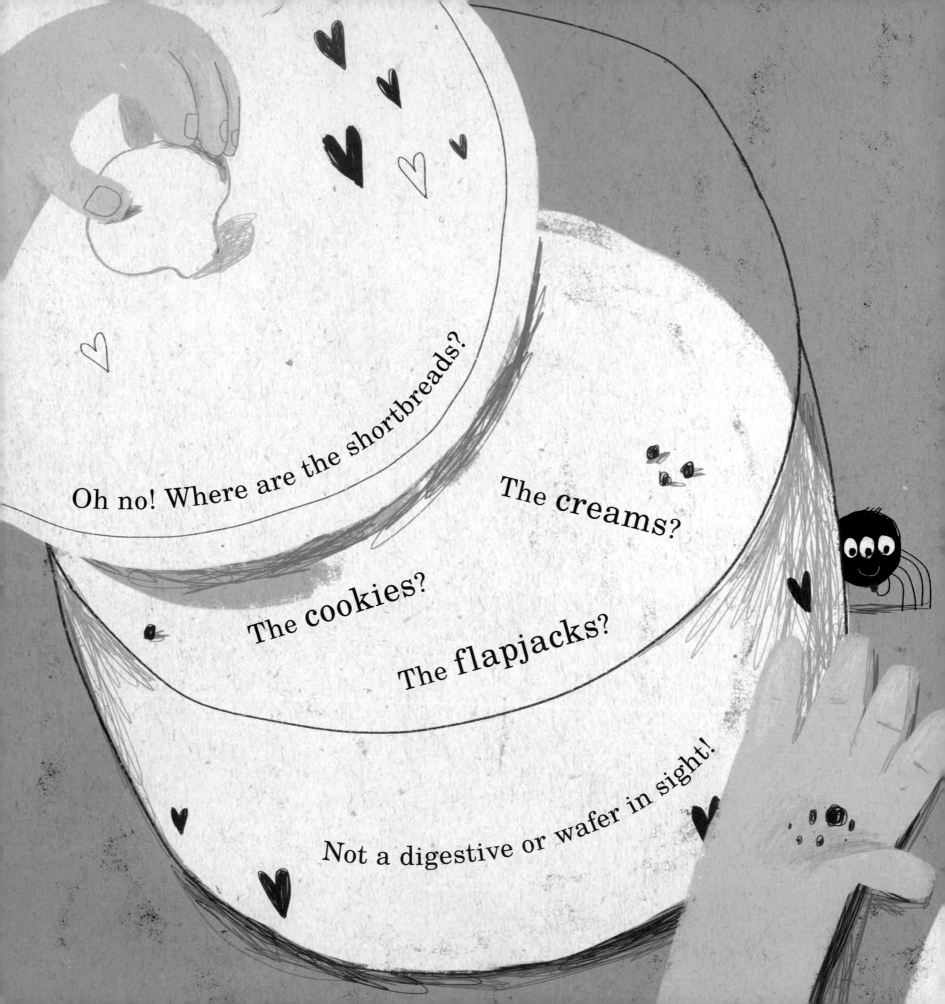

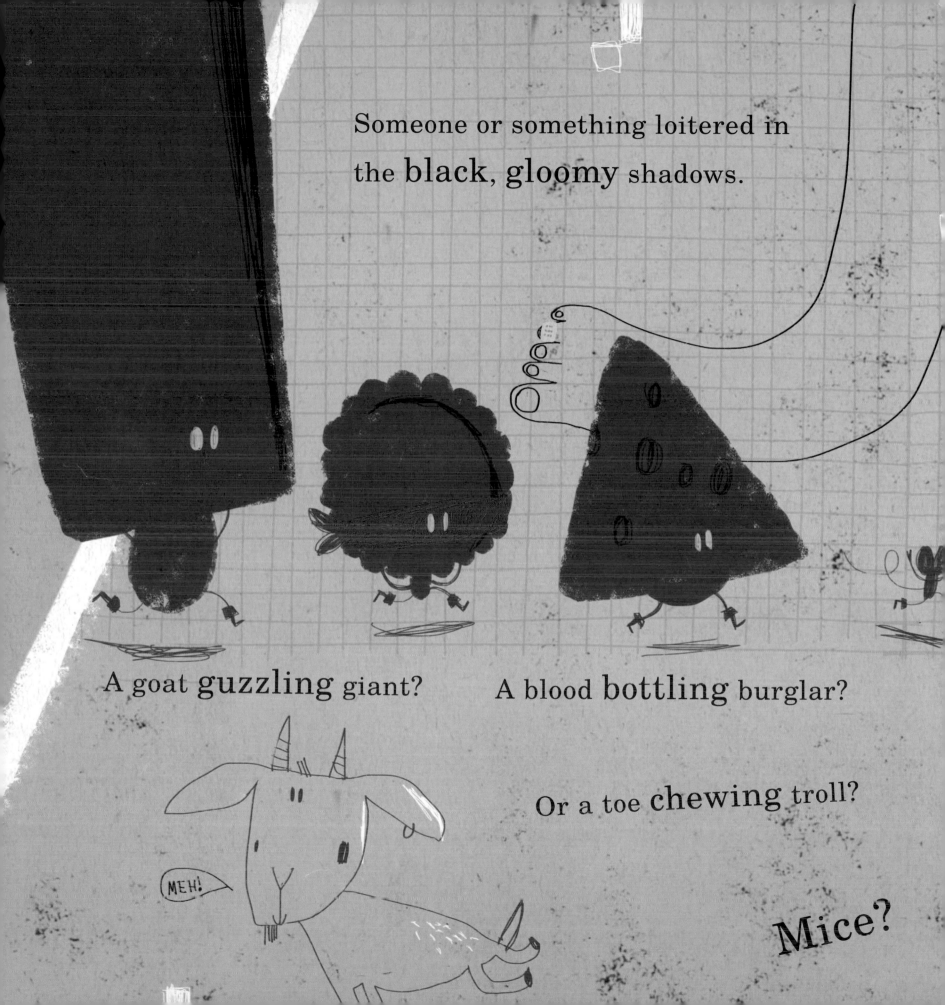

Someone or something loitered in the black, gloomy shadows.

A goat guzzling giant?

A blood bottling burglar?

Or a toe chewing troll?

MEH!

Mice?

Mischievous, squeaky, sneaky pirate mice scuttling away Oliver's biscuits!

Hauling and heaving,
towing and tugging.

Where were they going?

To the garden!

Where the legendary Sneaky McSqueaky roared,

"Aahaarrrr, me squeakies! Great work!"

But the pirate mice were not eating the biscuits...

The pirate mice were making...

Rockets!

Aerodynamic biscuit rockets to fly to the moon!

Sneaky McSqueaky ordered, "Climb aboard! Let's get us some chedda**arrr**!"

But the flapjacks were too **heavy**.

The wafers, too **light**.

The shortbread was too **crumbly** and the

ones with nuts were terribly **uncomfortable**.

Just when the pirate mice thought all hope was lost...

He cut and he carved,
he scored and he sliced.

Strawberry Jam

He measured and marked and fastened until...

The Jolly Dodger was ready for take off!

"Destination moon."

"Five... four... three...

Into the dark sky they **whooshed**, whizzed, zoomed

and landed on the **round, cheesy** moon.

They **drilled** and **dug** and **chiselled** and **chopped.**
They **quartered** and **cubed** and **cut** up until...

Grrrrrrrrrrrrrrrrrrrrrrrrrr

...their tummies couldn't wait another second!

Where is Sneaky McSqueaky?
Mouseknapped?

By a cheese chomping giant?

By a tail crunching troll?

Or a mouse crushing martian?

That mischievous, squeaky, greedy pirate mouse
was polishing off the biscuit rocket!

Chewing and chomping, guzzling and gulping.

"How are we going to get home?"

"You're pirates!" said Oliver,
"What you need is a...

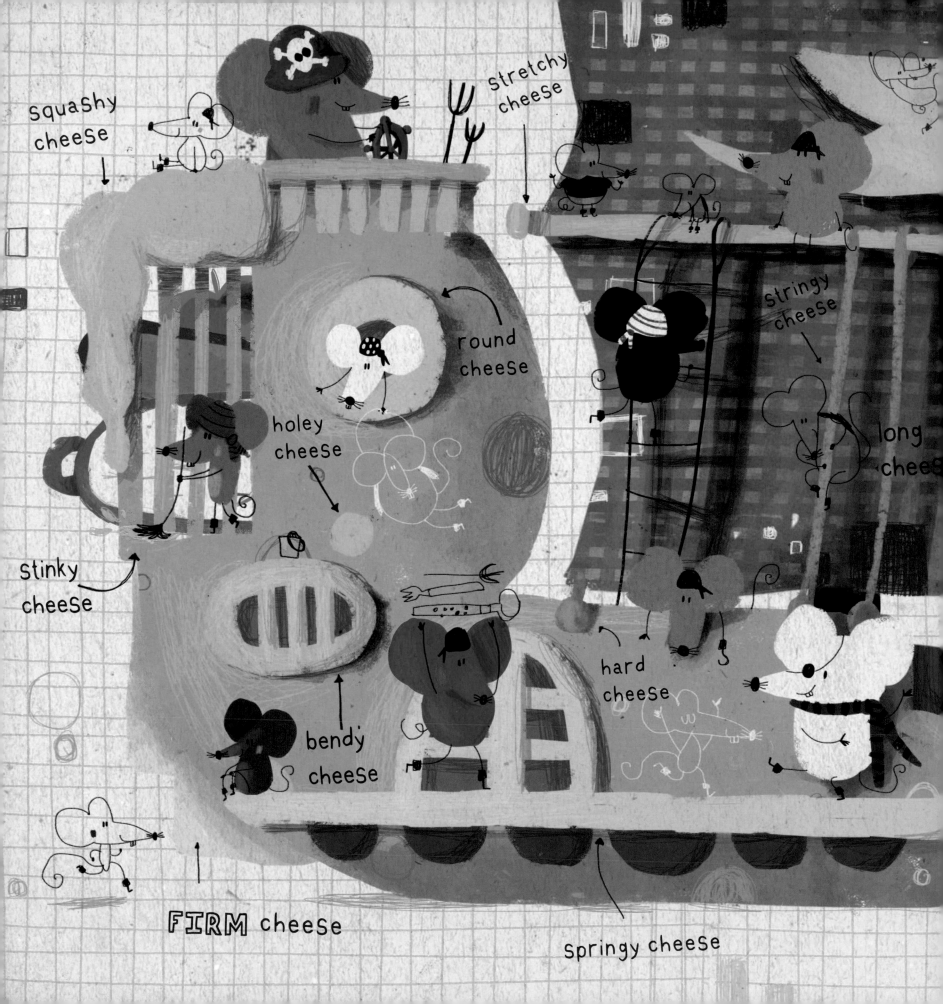

SHIP!

"An aerodynamic pirate ship to steer you to earth! We don't have biscuits but we do have **cheese**!

Soon the Brie O'Booty was ready to launch!

"Hoist the sail, me squeakies!"

Into the dark,
dark sky they
glided, floated,
drifted until...

"Land ahoy!"

"Phew!"

...they arrived safe and
sound in Oliver's garden.

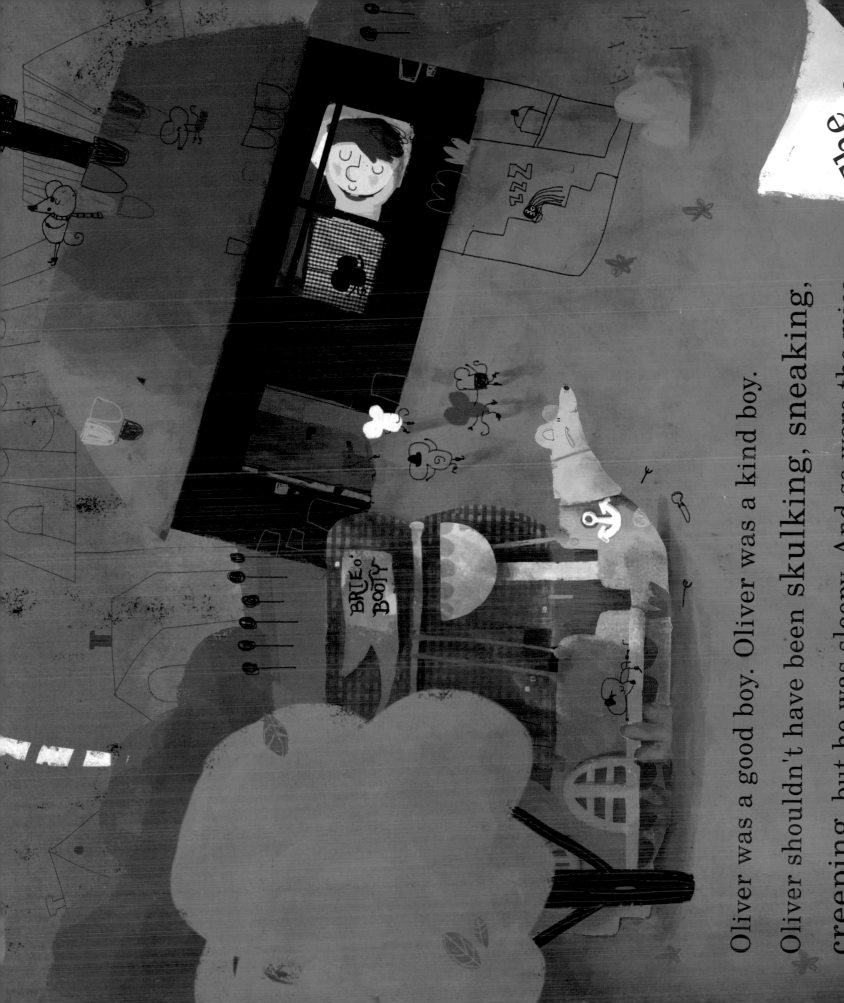

Oliver was a good boy. Oliver was a kind boy.

Oliver shouldn't have been skulking, sneaking,

creeping, but he was sleepy. And so were the mice.

The End?

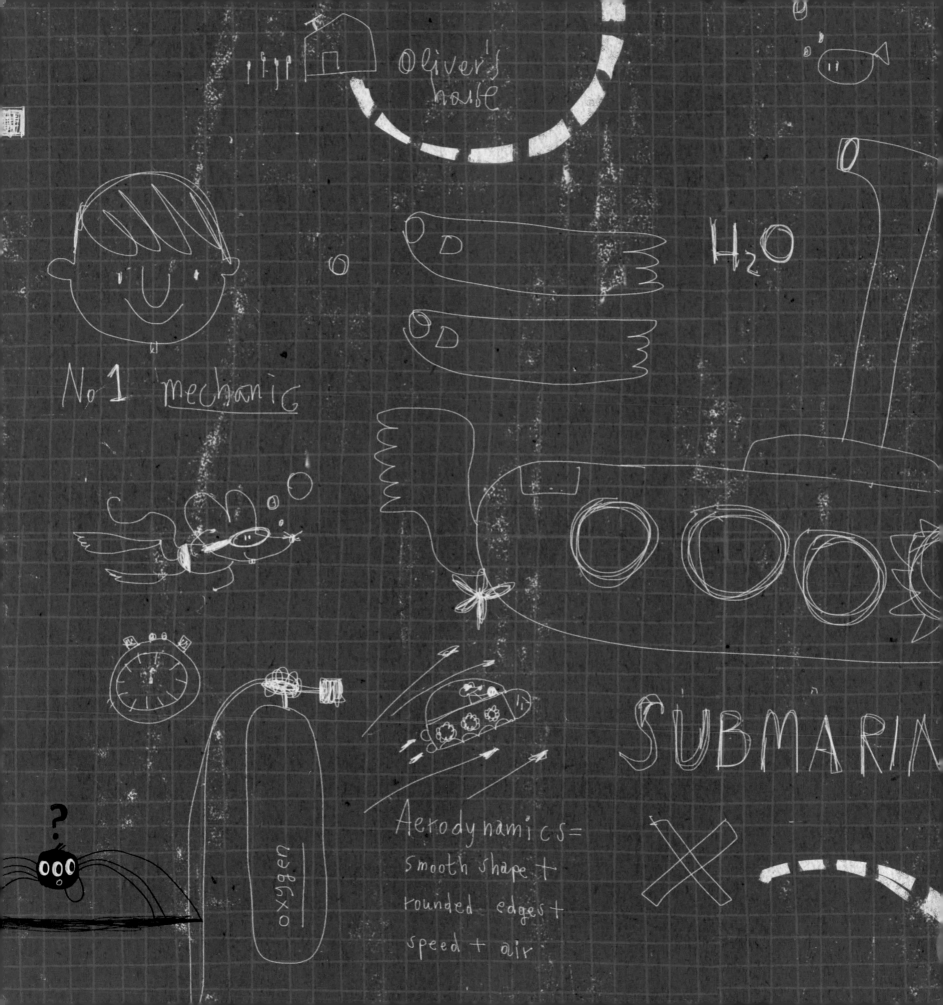

Oliver's house

No1 mechanic

H₂O

SUBMARIN

oxygen

Aerodynamics=
smooth shape +
rounded edges +
speed + air

Well, maybe not
all of them!

Aerodynamics of Biscuits

An original concept by author Clare Helen Welsh

© Clare Helen Welsh

Illustrations by Sophia Touliatou

Published by MAVERICK ARTS PUBLISHING LTD

Studio 3A, City Business Centre, 6 Brighton Road,

Horsham, West Sussex, RH13 5BB

© Maverick Arts Publishing Limited September 2015 +44 (0)1403 256941

A CIP catalogue record for this book is available at the British Library.

ISBN 978-1-84886-181-7

www.maverickbooks.co.uk

Maverick
arts publishing